Intro: "Filling The Void"

    Since I was a child, right around the age of 6,

I knew I was not the same as ordinary girls. The kind

of conversations I was having with myself about what

was going on inside of me would be considered

uncommon, to say the least. I enjoyed being a little

girl who stood up to pee on many occasions...

It felt good; it felt comfortable!

I'd miss my penis though; a partial incompleteness

would come over me every time I'd look down. It left

me wanting to know why I didn't have it anymore, or

why I couldn't see it. Because, in my brain, I felt in a sense, I was supposed to have one all along, and I have been searching towards fixing it; even if it's just to satisfy my mind.

Anatomically, my vagina is precisely where it's supposed to be; but, my dick, someone just seemed to have misplaced it this time around; so, I bought one! Matter of fact, I bought several of them, trying them ALL on for size.

This transition into womanhood continues to blossom for me though. I enjoy catching glimpses of myself whenever I pass by a mirror in the nude — often aroused simply by admiring my own body, and exploring what makes me feel good. I've practiced satisfying myself in so many ways, and I've gotten good at knowing what I like, and understanding how my mind processes who I am, inside and out.

Last week, I met Marq. I won't be able to take him seriously if he has difficulty accepting who I am, or if sex is his sole interest. But hey, that's sorta cool too… because I enjoy the way, the scent of my panties arouses him.

Chapter One

He saw me walking coming up the hill, wearing my crisp white sundress; I'd just gotten it too! I'm not one for high fashion or brand names, but this dress had some style to it, some class about itself. I had fancied it at Lenox Mall and seemed to wear it well. You should've seen him staring me down from head to toe. A scene straight out of one of those thirst-quenching commercials, followed by a slow-motion panoramic kind of shot; thirsty self, licking his lips and everything. Wearing this Big Ole Sticker on his arm-band, saying: "Get Tested!"

Once our eyes finally met, after I had gotten thru eyeballing, and mentally snap chatting his broad shoulders, firm chest, and luscious lips. Oh my gawd, his lips gave me thoughts of an indecent proposal. I should not have been thinking the things I was thinking, in the manner in which I was feeling them, AND I didn't even know his name yet...nor his sign.

I mean, we still ask: "so what's your sign?" Right?

Isn't it like a rule or something?

RULE: Before suck-facing; ask sign!

Listen, it had been a while since a man piqued my in-thrust the way he did. Without exchanging a single word, he aroused a tingling sensation inside of me. His presence illuminated a secret path into the base of my loins, around the taint region; and, it felt invigorating! It's an acquired mental condition, and he popped the tin wide-open with that; "Please, let me help you!"

His co-workers on the base seemed to get a kick outta watching him, 'handle himself,' but either way, it was a treat for me to witness him grin cheek to cheek. The way his eyes went stalking my thighs, taunting my flesh underneath; thoughts of watching him devour

this sweet, Georgia Peach. Well, truth be told; I'm not

actually from Georgia. I replied, "My my, such lovely

customer service. Is everyone greeted with that

awesome smile, because I'm feeling quite privileged."

I promise you, I heard him say with his eyes:

You're welcomed to have your way with me.

As I walked over towards the counter, he followed

closely behind. I spoke to him over my shoulder

regarding the whereabouts of a specific type of

pressure washer, but, by the time we had finally

gotten to the register, I'd realized I would only end

up repeating everything I had already said.

He stood at the counter, pulled out his pen, and a request form, looked up at me, smiled, and said; "I'm glad I came to work today. I was gonna go AWOL for a day, or say I was sick, or something...I would've missed out." Immediately I asked him, "Y'all on commission?" He responded, "No. I'm on salary. You know the military doesn't pay commission to us pawns."

He continued by telling me he'd just had a son, and didn't know he was a father until after the baby was already born. He was stationed in another part of the state and was transferred after he came back from his deployment. He started to get too deep into some outrageous Maury baby mamma drama madness, and the quickest way to get me uninterested, is to start telling me about all of your; "JERRY, JERRY" episodes! So, as you can imagine, I was beginning to lose interest in him quickly.

He asked one or two tidbits about me: My name, contact number, address, email, and when do I want it. Well, you know, working from that last question, the answer would sound something like:
Right now, and screw all the formalities. But, you

know I couldn't say that out loud, right? I mean, come on — Yet secretly, everything in me wanted too! I wanted to go full no holds barred, and add:

Sure you're a pretty face, but it is a fact; individuals who work well under pressure, and those who are open to new ideas, are found more useful in modern day society. How useful are you? Let's cut thru the chase!

When I looked at it without all of my internal mind chatter, his questions were merely basic questions in answering the questionnaire. So, to avoid coming off as brash, I took a detour, and I asked him if he'd seen

Narnia, and what he'd experienced the moment Lucy entered the Wardrobe… if he would've gone in if he was her? He blurted out, "YES…Yes, Ma'am! Life is about experiences!" I wondered if he'd realized Lucy had no idea what she was getting into when she uncovered that unanticipated adventure.

Then, he asked me if he could use my number to get to know me better. He was looking for someone he could "open up to" without any strings, or attachments. If he only knew how many strings, and attachments my life entailed; he would've probably headed for the hills.

So I replied with, "feeling is mutual."

Consider me a therapist; my thoughts are this simple:

If you are happy being used, then consider yourself

useful. Obviously, I'm on a mission to get some ass-

istance, and maybe he is too. Over the years, I've

learned; pressuring someone to want as much as you

do, usually never works out exactly the way you want

it too. They have to want it just as much as you do, or

more.

The PX Manager approached chest upright, and an

awful strut, as if he was stuck marching in drill

formation. He reminded me of Foghorn Leghorn.

He'd come over to see if everything was under control, and wanted to assure me; that if Marq weren't "up to par," he'd hafta step in, and take over.

Now, if this severely gray and over the hill Rooster, was let's say; anyone as debonaire as a particular former U.S. national security advisor. Or even as cute and cuddly as the leader of that part of Asia hardly anyone is allowed to travel in and out of, then maybe, this would've been interesting on all sorts of levels. However, I had my sights set on the way Marq was LL'n, and Cool J'n his lips, and all kinds of neat treats that could be in store for me.

Chapter Two

I received a text in the evening from Marq, with a pic attached. Oh my gosh, he's so adorable, sporting those suckable lips; Yum! I'm sure he'd sent a selfie-focused on his luscious on purpose. What a tease — Followed by another text; asking me when was I going to have the pressure washer picked up, or did I need it delivered.

I thought of having him deliver it, that way, I could get a two-for-one. But, the delivery fee was over the cost of the rental, Soooo, that would not have been a wise choice. Plus, I didn't want to waste time with

this guy, especially if he wasn't going to pony up to

my liking.

"I'll have it picked up," I replied. "By who, who's

gonna pick it up?" "My Dad; in two days," I

responded. "Oh—ok, what kinda vehicle does he

drive?" I sighed and said, "A pick-up! A Burgundy

Chevy Pick-Up; An older 80's model with BIG balls

strapped to the hitch. You can't possibly miss him!"

He joshed, "your Dad, he's a wild guy."

An entire evening of frivolous text-messaging back

and forth, until he finally asked me to send a selfie, and when I responded with: "come take it yourself," seemed to have kicked the adventure up a notch! Look, It wasn't even 10 pm yet, and I was in my Drake mood. Some good head, in this comfortable bed, sounds about right on any night.

"Can't come tonight, Daddy Duty."

See now, I know I should be very understanding during these types of situations, even while experiencing blue balls! No one can tell me it's impossible for a woman to experience the agony of the defeat. I messaged him back with: "how does a

man cure blue balls, and will it work for a woman?"
His response, "If you can bear to wait until tomorrow
— I can show you." This sorta remoisten my thoughts
and my desires.

I have to remember to ask him what are his thoughts
on submission. I need to make it clear to him what I
want; No if's, and's, only butts! Most guys aren't open
to what I like as a woman, they think all women are
the same, and intimacy is only performed one way. I
mentioned this in one of our previous text messages.
He said he wants to let down his guard and feels he
can handle my abstract way of thinking; this is what

made him want to text me on a personal level.

By the way, I jokingly sent him a snapshot of my recent physical, and test results, with: "Hey Marq, you wanna do me?" He replied, "YES, PLEASE!" GOTUM...lol, That was the perfect answer...

"Let me do you first," was my response! Some more back and forth until the glass cracked! "Do me how? You're freakier than I thought," followed by; "I'm not gay."

I did not respond — I'd fallen asleep.

Awoke to several more messages from him, up thinking about our conversations, and asking me to delete the convo thread. This prompted me to lose my luster shortly before breakfast until he messaged me at 8 am with: "Good Morning Beautiful." I smiled and instantly felt Victory sliding in.

Later that evening, he'd meet me at the laundry-mat. A storm was passing over the city, and the pressure washer pick-up would have to be postponed until Monday. His other excuse for needing to see me was because; he wanted to make sure I was gonna get home safely. He'd taken my bags, and placed them in the Rav-4 he pulled up in. He opened the front door

for me to get in, and I automatically noticed how

clean the inside was — detailed clean.

I almost wanted to place down some paper, as to not

dusty the floor mats; it's something about a tidy man

that tickles my pickle. The compliments kept pouring

out onto him unintentionally. I saw him bursting with

pride; however, I couldn't help but wonder if he was

all in. By the time I navigated him to my place, I was

saturated with thoughts, anticipation — and then

some!

He handed me his phone, just as we were pulling up and told me to click the link. I found it a bit strange for a second until I noticed it was a link to his test results; no STD's detected.

After handing him back his phone in silence, we gathered the bags and walked inside the house to meet total darkness. The power was out, and it was pitch black. The wind was starting to pick up, and the breeze was filled with hot air.

We were both sweating from toting the bags, as we made our way inside. But, you better believe, as soon as he dropped the laundry bags off of his shoulders,

and onto the floor, I pulled him by the shirt, and

finally kissed him; sucked on his bottom lip, Oh yes I

did; I needed it! His breath was fresh, his tongue

smooth, and clean, as he slid it across my top lip.

Those lips of his cushioned mine comfortably.

After a few minutes of intense suck-facing, he gently

pulled away, chuckled, and said, "I'm a Libra!"

Just as our eyes adjusted to the darkness, he scooped

me up, tossed me over his shoulder; as we made our

way down the hall towards my bedroom, it gave me

the giggles for a little bit! He rested me across the bed

and slid his hands up my dress, gently spreading my legs apart. When a streak of lightning momentarily lit the room, it gave us a clear sneak peek of each other. It was apparent he was aroused, and I got to see the excitement visibly growing down his right pant leg.

Before I could close my legs, he pulled me closer towards the edge of the mattress, as if ready to ravage his next meal. The way he looked at me as he uttered; "please, let me taste you." It gave me butterflies, and instinctively, I obliged by reverting my unnoticeable resistance, slowly spreading my legs wide open, while tilting my hips upward towards his grin.

You should've seen the cheesy smile on my face!

It had been a while since I allowed anyone to touch

me, to taste me, to please me this way. After he had

gotten on his knees, he immediately buried his face

between my legs, sucking on my already dampened

cotton crotch; enticing my clit with his lustful,

talented tongue.

I felt when it magically slid my underwear to the side,

setting his sights on the Beaver Dam! His nose was

rubbing up and down on my sensitive flesh, his

hands scooping my hips with a firm grip. I'd be

remiss if I didn't mention that; I was sporting a little

peach fuzz. Don't judge me — I didn't know he was going to scoop me up from the laundry-mat; plus, my peach fuzz was pretty and neat.

I could feel satisfaction building when his tongue stiffened, and he began slurping juices out of me. Just before I was about to grab hold of his head, and drench his face; he flipped me over, and went into town. His nose heading for where the Sun didn't shine, while his tongue dug into my pot of golden treasure!

Marq's hands cupped my firm, round ass like;

gripping two melons, and seeing him throb from this

angle, only made me want him more. So, I offered to

return the pleasures; after being tipped, and tossed

with courtesy!

But first, I had to pee.

Chapter Three

I've often watched the way "Superhead" givers give head — And, it's because of the Super Heads of this world, why I've even remotely taken an interest in the art of fellatio. Once you become in-tuned with the art, your intuition flourishes into something magical! Foreplay and oral sex is an extension of intimacy. And, it should be practiced, as well as enjoyed; thoroughly.

After I peed and called him in to shower with me, I watched him undress like an animal. Stomping on his pant leg to get his foot outta the jeans; his boxer briefs

hugging his buns, and his shlong sitting well tucked,

and cozy. I had already slipped out of my halter dress

I wore to the laundry earlier, including those sticky

panties.

When he came in, he ushered me into the shower, and

immediately, before I could even turn the water on, I

felt a warm stream spewing down the curve of my

back — over my sacrum, between my crack, and

straight down to the tip of my coccyx — No warning!

In fact; he seemed tickled by my un-daunting facial

expression staring back at his reflection thru the

shower glass. I'd only hope he'd be able to handle it

when his butt would come up against something

hard, and it's his turn to embrace the moment.

"The body wash is a little fruity, but there are

essential oils in it that will moisturize your skin

nicely," I mentioned, as I began to set the water

temperature. "Don't make it too hot!" He bellowed, as

I aimed the handle in that direction; just in time too!

I love the water HOT, and possibly third-degree

potential burns for any unsuspecting amateur.

He started to get a chubby when I turned around to

lather up his chest and neck. The way he procured my waist while pulling my hips closer to meet his leaning tower of Pisa; confirmed my next move. He was ready, and so was I — Funny how I didn't realize he was uncircumcised until this very moment.

While in the shower, his eyes remained closed most of the time; so, I didn't attempt the real in-depth things I wanted to do. And; to be forthright, I've come to appreciate the convenience of sex in the shower. However; he seemed a little nervous, or maybe it was just me, reading too much into nothing at all. I needed to stop thinking so much and focus on baiting him...

I meant bathing him. I had to get him to follow me out of the shower, and over to the sink; in the dark. I wasn't expecting the power to come back on any time soon, and the way the lightning outside was illuminating the bathroom; the evening would be made for a memorable time, at least for one of us.

A little eager myself, and even though I wanted to take my time to enjoy the shower with him, my mind was racing; all I wanted to do was satisfy the craving. Whether there was a possibility he was indeed curious or not; he was only minutes from being backed into another world.

Lathering him up was a joy, with keen attention paid around his private parts; if you know what I mean. We thoroughly took pleasure in washing each other's bodies.

The moment I started stroking him while he was kissing me, his breathing sped up. My left hand slid down his back and wedged itself between his cheeks. My right hand caressed his balls ever so slightly, and with every stroke, I felt him hold his breath; just a little. If he was nervous now, he was in for a surprise in three, two, one!

My middle finger found an entryway, and his excitement spiked, spontaneously! With his head thrown back; he opened his mouth like a vampire would, and embedded his face into my neck. His balls started to spasm in my hand, and the head of his dick jerked.

I synchronized my rhythm, and honed in on the sounds he started making. His oscillating moans were trickling down my spine, triggering my sphincter muscle to contract, and my phantom anaconda to stand at complete attention.

The sounds of him cum'n intermittently, between the

claps of thunder, heightened my sensations.

Then, he nut'd — all over my bearded gem.

He grasped my face between both hands,

passionately kissing me, and for a moment, time

seemed to have been suspended.

Once I'd come to, I gave myself a good rinse off:

After motioning towards the shower exit, I reached

over and grabbed the towel off the rack. In an attempt

to take my time, patting myself dry, I was able to

admire him through the mirror on the wall.

The flow of the water in that shower is pretty intense.

It's been designed that way for several reasons, but I could tell he was enjoying the massive raindrop feature. The pressure is amazing! It's kinda like standing under a gushing waterfall, and while it cascades over you, it feels as if it penetrates through your back, vibrating into you like a beating drum, and he was enjoying it; Or, so it appeared.

On second thought, it's possible he could have been in slight shock. Your conclusion may be better than mine. I was in selfish mode and wasn't focused on anything else besides what was about to happen next.

I wrapped the towel around my chest after drying off and slipped on my packer. She had arrived a few weeks before I met Marq, and she was being held in a satin pouch, in the bathroom cabinet, under the sink, and Victory is her name.

You have to test them out ya' know. You can't just use any and any ole probe! I prefer Cyberskin myself personally, and the condom peaking outta the back pocket of his jeans was about to come in very handy. I'm not into sex with gay men; so luckily, he made it clear; he's straight.

My gaze over to him lingered. T'was something captivating about the way he bent his head forward; the water was dripping off his chin, and the tip of his nose — water streaming from his retracted foreskin, like a moving piece of artwork.

I'm pretty sure tonight will be the first time he will have ever experienced being sucked quarter-back style! I washed him up good, from head to toe, front to back. And; the moment he allowed me to slide my hand up and down between his bum, instantly set off a range of fireworks inside my brain. It reminded me of the favor I needed to repay him from earlier; when he had me faced down, ass up in the air — So now, it was his turn.

Once I'd stooped down to slip on the condom under my towel, he glanced over to see what I had been toying with. He wasn't able to see much of anything, besides the jar of coconut oil; I had on the countertop, left opened. I grabbed his hand, and pulled him closer; proceeding to dip his hand into the glass jar. "It's Organic," I proclaimed, as I pulled it out.

Immediately, I manipulated his hand under mine and used his palm to ultimately stroke him solid.

The smirk on his face seemed to slowly build as I

motioned him over the basin, gently tipping him

forward; with his face pressed up against the mirror.

Prepped and ready, I proposed; he, 'Stop Me!'

In that instance, my stomach started to knot up, and

my throat tightened. The craving was real, and I was

in the midst of feeding the hunger. The coconut oil

was still within reach, and I wanted this to be as

smooth sailing as possible. I mean hey, comfortability

is vital — Right? So, I lubed him up well and good,

even massaged his back for a little — while working

my way to his slightly hairy bum; adjusted myself a

bit, took aim, stuck out my tongue, and went in for some fun.

His gasp gave him away!

The first time you get a tongue up your ass will always be something you will forever remember. Well, unless you develop Alzheimer's, or amnesia, or something like that; but, other than that — you're bound to remember the first time you get a tongue up the bum.

He tried to brace himself from pressing his face too hard into the mirror; he was busily fogging up with his uneven panting. Unbeknownst to him, he was in for another awakening. A few seconds later, my magic thumb replaced my tongue, allowing me to get to some sucking. Duly noted was his groan when the switch occurred.

After I positioned his left knee up onto the counter, I was able to pull his cock back to meet with his ball sack. Now; with this front row view from behind the scene, I was able to sumo squat, and toss his salad the proper way. Do all men love their jewels licked, and sucked this way — Ever so carefully, with purpose, and tender vigor?

With both bags carefully secured, and wholly occupying the space in my skull cave, I could feel him swelling to a tightness. I'd long for the feeling of a thick cock down my throat; and by the looks of it, he wouldn't be able to handle it for too much longer, and I wasn't ready for him to cum just yet; at least not like this. So, I slowed to a suckling stop, stood up, and considerately conveyed my intention:

With a slight seductive whisper, I said, "get ready."

My thoughts were clear and focused. Execute commencement with Victory as safely, and pleasurable as possible.

Our eyes immediately locked in the mirror when he felt Victory press up against him, and slowly started to gain entry. His eyebrows tightened, as I pressed into him again, just a notch; drizzling a little more oil between us, I told him to; "stop me." Instead, he closed his eyes, tilted his chin upward, and sighed with a wincing squint. Pretty confident this was his first encounter of this kind; he appeared determined to please me!

My thighs took a few minutes before it met the back of his. Luckily for him; coconut oil is a versatile lubricant, and it smelled pleasant between our skin.

He attempted to restrain me; slightly, when my excitement increased, and I was already all the way in. He began squeezing my thigh, as a sign, or something; I wasn't sure. Truthfully, it only excited me more, and caused the walls of my pussy to contract, and pulsate!

A few more minutes into driving Victory home, and he started to "Superman" himself. It kept squirting out; globs of it. The look of it sliding down his leg quenched a lingering appetite filled by that all familiar cum smell I'd miss, but remembered, oh so very well.

And; if you'd ask me, I shot my proverbial load way into him, about the same time he'd skeet'd down his thigh, and all over the cabinet doors, and bathroom floor.

After we cleaned up, he wanted us to cuddle.

I wasn't sure if it was for him, or for me; because, 90 seconds after hitting the pillow, he was fast asleep; snoring! But, at least it gave me a chance to think about how well Victory stood up. This was my first time breaking her in; my other straps are much bigger than this one. It was his first time, and her first time out the box — she's only 5.5 inches; Sweet Victory!

Pawn? Maybe eventually he can be upgraded! His head game is well above pawn moves; but, he's no Knight; at least not yet. Only time will be able to tell what other parts he will play in my pursuit of a deserving King. Settling down is part of my plan; so, who knows what the future holds.

I let him sleep till midnight; woke him up to an Italian sub sandwich, and an Arnold Palmer. "You ok?" I asked him in the middle of his yawn. "Sit up, eat something; it's getting late, and the storm is getting heavier." While in the middle of scarfing down the sub, he commented on having been more prepared, so he could have spent the night.

Honestly, I was ready for him to go. The kind of intimate overnight stay I'm interested in does not include anyone falling asleep so quickly. A woman like me needs more than just a few minutes.

After walking him to his vehicle, and getting a very intense goodnight kiss; he gushed on it all being an experience of his lifetime. All I could think about was how long this two-piece snack would fill me up for, and when would I be getting some more.

The first thing the next morning, a voice message

arrived at 6:51 from Marq.

He said, "Last Night Was Amazing!"